WHOEVER HEAR
ON OAK

After school Mark and ___ ___ ___ue
building. This time we saw a crowd of kids in front.

Half our sixth-grade class marched along the sidewalk. No joking, laughing, poking each other, teasing, or snatching baseball caps and throwing them
around in games of keepaway. Just kids, marching
quietly.

There was something spooky about it.

If we walked right up with the other kids, maybe
we could get inside without making the guard suspicious.

I grabbed Mark's arm. "Come on." We approached
the door behind the last of the Two Ts kids. . . .

I held up the key card. . . .

I ran the card through the slot.

The door swung open.

Mark and I stepped through—and into another
world.

R.L. Stine's
Ghosts of Fear Street®
#30

I WAS A
SIXTH-GRADE
ZOMBIE

A Parachute Press Book

A GOLD KEY PAPERBACK
Golden Books Publishing Company, Inc.
New York

A GOLD KEY PAPERBACK Original

Golden Books Publishing Company, Inc.
888 Seventh Avenue
New York, NY 10106

I Was a Sixth-Grade Zombie written by Nina Kiriki Hoffman

ISBN: 0-307-24901-8

First Gold Key Paperback printing May 1998

10 9 8 7 6 5 4 3 2 1

Cover art by Happy Boy Pat

Printed in the U.S.A.

Chapter ONE

"**I** don't get it," I said to my best friend, Mark. I gazed around my empty basement. "This is supposed to be the best show yet. It's got albino worm creatures as big as humans! Where *is* everybody?"

On Wednesday afternoons after school, my basement fills with kids. They come to watch my favorite TV show of all time, *Strange Cases*. It's about two investigators for a secret agency. They check out weird paranormal stuff.

It usually turns out to be even weirder than they think.

Strange Cases actually runs at ten P.M. on Tuesday nights. Most of us are in bed by then. Or at least we're not allowed to be watching TV that late. So I tape it and show it Wednesday afternoons on my VCR.

We have a great time watching it. We munch on microwave popcorn. We rewind and look at the weirder stuff in slo-mo. We argue about whether it could ever really happen.

I kind of think most of it could. See, I live on Fear Street, in the town of Shadyside. Weird things happen on Fear Street. Creepy things. People say they've seen ghosts there—and worse.

I've never seen anything weird. But I'm still hoping.

Mark and I haven't told anyone, but we want to be investigators when we grow up.

Anyway, when we watch *Strange Cases*, we all have lots to talk about.

But last week only three people besides Mark showed up.

And this week it was only Mark and me.

What was going on?

Mark took a gulp of cream soda. He loves that stuff. Gross!

"Come on, Valerie," he urged. "Let's start the tape."

"But, Mark, where *is* everybody?"

Mark stuffed a handful of popcorn in his mouth before he answered. He's always hungry.

Mark is one of the shortest boys in our sixth-grade class. I'm one of the tallest girls. We've been best friends since third grade, when we were both the same size.

Mark has short black hair, dark tan skin, and a space between his front teeth. He wears wire-rimmed glasses. And he's very quiet.

I have strawberry-blond hair and freckles. And a big mouth. I'm the opposite of Mark. Maybe that's why we're such good friends.

"Mph phmbf mmph," Mark said.

I poked him. "What?"

Mark swallowed. "Let's phone them."

I grabbed the phone and dialed A.J. Hilton's number.

"Who are you?" A.J.'s little brother, Bart, screamed over the phone.

I held the receiver away from my ear. "A friend of AJ's," I hollered back. No one can outscream me! "Where is he?"

"Ow, my ear! At his dumb club!" Bart slammed the phone down.

I told Mark what Bart said. "What club?" he asked.

"I don't know. I thought *this* was our club. The *Strange Cases* Club," I answered, frowning.

Weird.

We tried Elaine Costello's number next. Her mom answered. "Oh, of course, Valerie," she said. "Elaine joined the M-W Club. Aren't you in it?"

"Uh—no," I told her. I hung up, puzzled. "Have you ever heard of the M-W Club?" I asked Mark.

"Don't you remember? The afterschool clubs Mr. Hool started. The Monday-Wednesday Club and the Tuesday-Thursday Club. He called them M-W and Two Ts."

"Oh, yeah," I muttered. "*Those* clubs. The loser clubs."

Mr. Hool was new. He started teaching at Shadyside Middle School after winter break. He wore thick diamond-shaped glasses that made his pale eyes look twice as big as normal. He was super-tall, too.

And he was always cold. In winter he walked around in three sweaters and a jacket—inside the school building! Now that spring was here, he cut back to two layers.

He had lots of ideas, including this one about the clubs. "Each one of you should join a club," Mr. Hool told us on his first day. "Maximize your brain power! Strengthen your bodies! Polish your manners! Become the best children you can be!"

I decided right then that this guy was a major weirdo. The clubs sounded *so* lame. Mark and I didn't even consider joining. As usual, we were in total agreement.

So how come everyone else joined?

How could kids pass up *Strange Cases* for some dumb club?

"Come on, Val," Mark said again. "If those guys want to miss *Strange Cases*, that's their problem. Start the tape."

"Wait. Let's try Steve Hickock first," I suggested. "He'd never join one of those clubs. He's way too cool."

Mark riffled through the phone book until he found the number. I dialed. Steve's mom picked up.

"Hi, Valerie," she said in a distracted voice. Steve's baby sister, Gretchen, wailed in the background. "Steve isn't home. He's off at some club."

I couldn't believe it! Steve too? How come our friends joined this dumb club and never even told me and Mark?

"Do you know where the club is?" I asked Steve's mom.

"On Oak Street, just past the bowling alley," she replied.

"Thanks." I put the phone down and made up my mind.

"Let's go check out this club," I said to Mark.

He stared sadly at the VCR for a minute. Then he nodded.

"Where did that come from?" Mark asked.

"I don't know. I never noticed it before." I stared

at the big pale-blue building on Oak Street. "How could I miss it?"

It was slick, almost see-through—but not quite. It looked like a giant ice cube. I shivered just looking at it. There was only one window—a tiny dark square right next to a pale yellow door. A uniformed guard sat scowling behind the glass.

As we watched, three kids marched up the sidewalk. One of them was Ginger Park. She smart-mouthed Mr. Hool in class that day. The other two pulled a fire alarm.

"Weren't they all given detention after school?" Mark asked.

I checked my watch. School let out half an hour ago.

"Maybe they got sent to the clubs instead of detention," Mark suggested.

I snorted. "Yeah. The clubs are so boring, they're worse punishment."

The kids stepped up to the yellow door. They unzipped their backpacks and took out what looked like credit cards.

One by one they stuck the cards into a slot on the door. A buzz sounded and the door opened for each kid.

"What do they *do* in there?" Mark wondered.

"Let's find out!" We crossed the street and approached the guard's window.

"Hi." I smiled. "Can we go inside?"

The guard frowned. "Your key cards are where?"

Key cards? He must mean those things the other kids used to open the door. "Uh—I forgot mine," I lied.

The guard glared at me. "No card, no entry."

I usually don't give up that easily. But for some reason I couldn't think of any arguments. I stared at the guard.

Luckily Mark tugged my arm and pulled me away.

Mark and I make a good team. When I'm brain-dead, he kicks into action. And vice versa.

We ducked around the corner. On this side the building was a flat blue wall two stories tall and a block wide. There wasn't a single window.

Mark's eyes were narrow. "It's sure got a lot of security for an after-school club." He reached toward the slick blue wall.

Before Mark's fingers actually touched the wall, his hand slipped sideways. "Whoa!" he exclaimed, and tried it again.

Again his hand slipped before he touched the surface.

Mark's eyes grew perfectly round. He turned and stared at me. "Val," he whispered. "I think that's a force field!"

"A *force field*?" The hair on the back of my neck prickled. "That's impossible!" I sputtered.

Force fields don't exist in *real* life, I thought. Only in sci-fi movies. Or TV programs like *Strange Cases*.

Mark grabbed my hand and pulled it toward the building. My hand was pushed back from the blue wall. By something invisible.

Mark was right. We were inches away from a force field.

We had just found our very own strange case.

Chapter TWO

"**W**hat kind of after-school club has a force field around it?" I shivered. "This place is creeping me out."

"No kidding," Mark agreed. "It—"

He broke off as heavy footsteps crunched toward us. Seconds later a policeman appeared around the side of the building. He glared down at us.

"What are you doing here?" he demanded.

"Just looking at this building," I replied. "Is that illegal?"

"Yeah, is that illegal?" Mark echoed. His voice squeaked a bit. I could tell he was scared. But at least he was sticking with me instead of running away.

Mark is a great friend, but he's—well, I have to

admit it: sometimes he's sort of chicken. I'm working on getting him to be braver. And he's trying to get me to think before I act.

The policeman frowned. He blinked a couple of times.

"No," he said. "Not illegal. It's just—not a good idea."

"Why not?" I asked.

"This place is a chemical warehouse." The policeman blinked some more. "It could be dangerous for citizens of the town."

He said the words flatly. As if he'd memorized the speech. Also, there was something sort of stretched out about his voice. Like a tape recording that's a little worn.

And what was with all the blinking?

I suddenly got a mental picture of a giant windup policeman with a big key in his back. An icy feeling zipped down my spine.

He patted my shoulder. "So just move along, there," he ordered, giving me a little shove.

"But—" Mark began.

"Yes, sir," I cut in. I grabbed Mark's arm and dragged him away. What a time for him to decide to argue!

As we left, I peeked over my shoulder at the police officer.

I didn't see any key sticking out of his back.

But I still couldn't shake the feeling that there was something weird about him.

"We'll come back later," I whispered to Mark. "We've got to find out more about this place!"

The next day Mr. Hool started class with a big announcement about a contest. As he talked, I studied my fellow students.

The three kids I saw going into that weird blue building didn't look sick or full of chemicals or anything.

Besides, I thought, that whole chemical-warehouse excuse didn't make sense. Why would an after-school club be held in a dangerous building. That policeman was lying for sure.

I checked out Steve and Elaine and AJ.

Normal. All normal.

"The students who write the top ten essays will win a week-long trip to Neverland," Mr. Hool said.

What an awesome prize! Neverland is a theme park about an hour away from Shadyside. It has colossal roller coasters and great scary rides—the kind that make you scream your head off.

I'm a pretty good writer. I was psyched to win the essay contest.

Then Mr. Hool finished his announcement.

"The title of your essay will be 'Why Good Manners Are Important to Everyone.'" He smiled at us. "You may use the rest of this class period to begin writing."

Good manners?

Yuck!

What can you write about good manners? I would *never* win!

I glanced at Mark to see if this topic irritated him as much as it did me. What does he know about manners? I mean, Mark is the class burping champion. He can burp the alphabet! And has been scolded plenty of times for it, believe me.

But he was staring at Mr. Hool with a dazed, hopeful look on his face. I guess he really wanted to go.

Mark got out his pen and some paper and started writing eagerly. He's the best writer I know. He can make anything sound good. Even a loser topic like good manners. He was sure to win.

Most of the other kids started writing, too.

I hunched over at my desk, fiddling with my pencil.

A shadow fell across me. I glanced up.

Mr. Hool towered above me, frowning. His eyes behind his diamond-shaped glasses looked enormous.

I sighed and got out some paper too.

During recess I caught up with Elaine Costello.

"So—you didn't come over to see *Strange Cases*," I said. I tried not to sound offended or anything. "What did you do at your club? Was it really more fun?"

"The M-W Club?" Elaine frowned and stared at her shoes. "It's a chess club."

"A *chess* club?" I exclaimed. "No way!"

Why would a chess club need a building with no windows, a guard at the door, electronic key cards, and a force field?

What were they afraid of? Someone would steal a pawn?

"How many kids are in the club?" I asked.

"Huh?" She blinked twice. "What are you talking about?"

Hello! Earth to Elaine! "Chess. At the M-W Club."

"Oh." She smiled at me and blinked some more. "Right. I love the M-W Club. It's so much fun. I wish I could go every day."

The hair on my arms started to prickle. It wasn't just the things she was saying—even though they did sound really lame. It was the way she was talking. Her voice seemed slower and a little deeper. *Stretched.*

Kind of like that policeman yesterday. Even the blinking.

I have got to see what's inside that building, I thought.

I need to know what these clubs are all about!

I thought for a second. Today was Thursday. "You won't be going back until Monday, right?" I asked Elaine. "So you won't be needing your key card. Can I borrow it?"

She squinched up her nose. "I guess," she replied slowly. She blinked again and shook her head, as if a fly were bothering her. She pulled the white key card out of her backpack and handed it to me. "But make sure you give it back before Monday."

"I will," I promised.

After school Mark and I headed for the big blue building. This time we saw a crowd of kids in front. It must be the Tuesday-Thursday Club—the Two Ts. I had no idea it was so popular!

Half our sixth grade class marched along the sidewalk. No joking, laughing, poking each other, teasing, or snatching baseball caps and throwing them around in games of keepaway. Just kids, marching quietly.

There was something spooky about it.

I gripped Elaine's key card. If we walked right up with the other kids, maybe we could get inside without making the guard suspicious.

I grabbed Mark's arm. "Come on." We approached the door behind the last of the Two Ts kids.

The guard watched everyone going in.

I held up the key card.

"Val," Mark whispered. "I'm kind of scared."

"Don't be chicken," I whispered back. But secretly I was nervous too.

I ran the card through the slot.

The door swung open.

Mark and I stepped through—and into another world.

Chapter THREE

The air in the building was thick, warm, and wet, like the air in the bathroom right after you've had a long, hot shower. It smelled flowery, but also a little like metal.

An empty corridor stretched out ahead of us, then curved. Troughs and pots of wild, leafy plants lined the pale green walls. I saw ferns, palm trees, orchids, and a lot of other plants I didn't recognize.

Above the plants, silver lace marked with red, green, blue, and purple bumps patterned the walls. It looked like computer circuit boards.

Panels of soft silver light covered the ceiling.

Oval doors lined the walls. They reminded me of the doors in submarines. None of them had knobs, or even those spinning wheels submarine guys use to open doors.

The Two Ts kids were nowhere in sight. They must have gone through one of the doors along the corridor, I guessed. Or around the corner.

I couldn't hear anything but Mark's and my breathing.

"This sure doesn't look like any chess club," I whispered.

"Maybe the whole building is a computer!" Mark said in a hushed voice. He stepped forward, peering at the walls.

I followed. "Whoa!" I exclaimed as my foot slid sideways. I glanced down.

The carpet looked like somebody's crew cut— short, hairy, brown-blond. It wasn't like a regular rug at all. It made for slippery walking.

Mark wiped sweat off his face with his sleeve. "I think these plants are tropical," he muttered, fingering one of the giant leaves. "This place is way weird."

"Tell me about it," I agreed.

"I have a bad feeling, Val. I think we should go."

"We can't go! I want to find out what's happening here!" I protested louder than I meant to.

"Shh!" Mark hissed.

"Sorry." I went on in a whisper. "You *always* have a bad feeling, Mark. What's the big deal? If someone catches us, we'll just say we're looking for our club and got lost. Now, let's get moving. I want to know if those kids are really playing chess. Or whatever the Two Ts are supposed to do."

"How can we even find them?" Mark argued. "They could be in any one of these rooms."

"Let's listen at the doors until we hear kids' voices. You take that side, and I'll take this," I told Mark.

He sighed. "Okay."

I crossed to the nearest door, a light-blue one. I put my ear against it. It felt cool and metallic.

All I could hear was a lot of clicking noises, like typewriter keys. Not the sound chess-playing kids would make, unless they moved the pieces really fast.

I headed up the corridor toward the next door on my side, then turned to glance at Mark. He had his ear to a door and his eyes squeezed shut.

"Hey!" a voice behind me said. "What are you doing here?"

I froze. My heart thudded.

All my arguments about how it was no big deal if we got caught suddenly seemed unconvincing. Who knew what they would do to us?

Who knew who *they* were?

We were about to find out.

Chapter FOUR

I turned around slowly and saw—

Trevor Dean!

It was only Trevor Dean!

My breath whooshed out of me in a shaky sigh. "Whew!"

Trevor was a new kid. He joined our class halfway through the year. I didn't really know him at all.

He was kind of geeky. I heard he was really good with computers. You could tell he spent a lot of time alone with them. He looked as if he never got any sunlight—totally pale skin, short white-blond hair, eyebrows, and eyelashes. And his clothes never quite fit. They were always just a little too small.

"What are *you* doing here?" I whispered.

"I asked you first!" Trevor shot back.

"Are you in the Two Ts?" Mark asked, coming up beside me.

Trevor paused, then shook his head.

"How about the M-W Club?" I pressed.

He shook his head again.

Well, that was something. Trevor might be geeky, but at least he wasn't geeky enough to join one of the clubs.

"We're checking out this whole club thing," I explained. "What do they do here? Why is there a guard on the door? What's with that weird force field around the building?"

"What is going on?" Mark added.

"Right." Trevor nodded. "I wondered the same thing."

"Do you know anything yet?"

"Not really." Trevor glanced nervously down the hall. "Do you?"

"We don't even know where the other kids went," Mark told him. "Did you see them come in? They were gone by the time we made it inside."

"I think they went that way." Trevor pointed toward the curve in the corridor.

"Let's go." I started down the hall, Mark right behind me.

"Wait," Trevor protested. "You can't just—I mean, I think this place might be dangerous!"

"Yeah. So?" I tried to sound as if I weren't scared.

"What if they catch you?" Trevor asked.

I glanced at Mark. He looked ready to bolt, but he didn't back toward the door. That made me feel braver. "What can they do? Throw us out? Big deal. I want to find out as much as I can before that happens."

Trevor thought that over for a minute. Then he shrugged. "Okay. Let's go."

I raised my eyebrows. I didn't remember inviting him along.

But this was a bad time to argue about it. Mark and I will straighten him out later, I decided.

We walked toward the curve in the corridor. I could hear some kind of weird music coming from an open door ahead. Once in a while a voice would murmur words I couldn't quite make out.

A whooshing sound to my right made me jump. My stomach clenched. I whipped my head to the side.

A lime-green door slid open. That was what made the noise. It worked like the doors on *Star Trek*, sliding to the side instead of opening out or in.

I held my breath. But no one came through the door. After a moment I ran over and peered into the room. Mark and Trevor followed me.

That bizarre silver lace with all the colored blobs in it covered the walls. Colored wires ran from the lace to a lot of strange, spiky machines that chugged softly.

We stepped over the raised threshold and gazed around.

"I feel like an ant inside a computer," Mark whispered.

A web of conveyor belts connected the machines. Small, silvery metal blocks rode the belts. Some of the blocks had spikes. Others had complicated patterns of holes. Each machine they passed added more spikes and holes and colored blobs.

A final conveyor belt dumped the strange little objects into a big bin in the middle of the room.

Wow!

No doubt about it. We had definitely found our very own strange case.

"What *is* this place?" I murmured.

"A factory," Mark said.

"Well, duhhh," I snapped. I mean, that was obvious. "But what is it making? Have you ever seen anything like this?" I crossed to the bin of metal things.

"Don't touch that!" Trevor yelled.

I jumped. Then I glared at him. He had both hands clapped over his mouth.

"Why not?" I demanded.

He lowered his hands. I'm sorry I yelled," he apologized. "But I don't think we should touch *anything* in here! We don't know what it does!"

"Yeah," Mark agreed. "It could be dangerous, Val."

What a pair of wimps!

I was over being nervous. We'd been in this weird building for more than five minutes, and we hadn't gotten into trouble yet.

"What could happen?" I scoffed. "They're just little pieces of metal. It's not like they're alive or anything."

I reached into the bin and grabbed one of the spiky objects. It was surprisingly light. I stared at it.

Before I could examine it, though, it—changed.

Silvery ribbons shot out and wrapped around my hand and fingers. Wires looped over the ribbons. Ribbons wove between themselves.

In about four seconds I had a silver glove on my right hand.

"Cool!" I exclaimed. I turned my hand this way and that, admiring the glove. It looked like something a heavy-metal rocker would wear. "Maybe I should get one for my other hand too."

Nobody else at school had one of these.

Then I realized I couldn't move my fingers.

And something tingly was happening to my palm.

Lacy silver wires stretched from the glove up my arm, wrapping around my wrist. They crept toward my elbow.

"Oh, no," I gasped. "What's happening?"

I tried shaking my hand, but the glove wouldn't come off.

I yanked on it with my other hand.

It wouldn't budge!

"Hey!" I stared at Mark and Trevor. I was starting to panic.

What if I could never get the glove off? I couldn't even use my hand! And—

"Val!" Mark cried suddenly. "Look out!" He pointed.

I glanced at the bin.

The rest of the little metal objects had stacked themselves into a tower.

And the tower was reaching for me!

Chapter FIVE

"**H**elp!" I cried.

A net of silver lace rattled from the tower, creeping across the floor.

The silver wires on my arm tightened. They swarmed up my shoulder.

Ribbons rose from the floor and swayed toward me like cobras. They were going to wrap me up into a silver mummy!

I'd never be able to move again!

"Help!" I shrieked again. "Help me!"

Trevor caught me by the shoulders and pulled me away from the reaching silver threads. Mark kicked at the silver ribbons on the floor, driving them back.

One of the ribbons wrapped around Mark's tennis

shoe. "Yai!" he yelped. He stood on one foot and jerked the other one against the ribbon.

It wouldn't break.

Oh, no! The silvery ribbons were trying to wrap us up like flies in spiderwebs!

Kicking furiously, Mark managed to peel the ribbon off his foot.

It struck at his hand like a snake.

"Aaaagh!" he yelled, stumbling backward.

"Run!" Trevor shouted. He dragged me toward the door. Mark ran for it too.

We all collided in the doorway.

"Get it off me," I begged, tugging at the wires on my arm.

Mark grabbed the wires and tried to unwind them. They began to wrap around his fingers!

"No!" he yelled, shaking his hand.

My glove sprouted little red, blue, and green buttons. Trevor started punching them frantically. Mark hit some too.

My whole hand tingled and burned.

All the buttons suddenly glowed bright. The glove split open down the middle.

Then it dropped off into Trevor's hands.

Trevor hurled it into the middle of the room, where the silver lace still sprawled and, crawled toward us. The lace grabbed the glove and oozed over it.

We didn't stick around to see what came next. We stumbled back into the corridor. The lime-green door whooshed closed.

I sagged to the floor. Mark and Trevor slumped beside me.

"Oh, man!" I groaned. "What just happened? What *was* that thing?"

"Who knows?" Trevor shook his head.

I swallowed hard. "Thanks for getting it off me."

"You're welcome," he answered. "Are you okay?"

"I think so." I examined my hand. It was pale, and tingled as if it were asleep. There was a red mark around my wrist.

I glanced at the others. Trevor's forehead was shiny, and Mark's glasses slipped down the bridge of his nose. We were all sweaty. The air was so hot and wet!

"Now what?" I asked.

Trevor raised his eyebrows at me. "I told you this place was dangerous. Don't you think we should get out of here?"

That was what I was about to suggest. But I can't stand it when people say "I told you so."

I guess that's what made me retort, "No way! What's so scary about a little wire? I want to find the other kids."

"After all that?" Mark asked. He didn't sound happy. He likes his excitement in small doses.

"Let's just look around that curve," I urged, point ing up the corridor. I flexed the fingers of my numbed hand. I was beginning to feel them again. "Then we can leave."

Mark sighed. And nodded. Trevor shrugged. We climbed to our feet.

"Come on," I commanded, and led the way.

I heard that music again. It was louder now.

It came from an open doorway down the corridor. Strange, soft synthesizer music with a slow bass beat. *Ba-BOOM! Ba-BOOM!* I could feel it right through my shoes. It was like a slow heartbeat.

"Let's go see what's in there," I whispered.

We tiptoed toward the open door. Light spilled out onto the corridor floor.

The closer I got, the more I felt as if the bass beat and my heartbeat were becoming one. It was creepy.

I sneaked closer, then knelt beside the door.

I peeked around the edge.

And I gasped.

Chapter SIX

Luckily, the music covered the sound of my gasp.

The room was full of kids—the other kids from our class.

But they weren't playing chess.

Or anything like it.

The kids stood in straight rows facing the front of the room. A tall woman in a shiny pink coverall gazed back at them.

"Sit," the woman commanded.

The kids all sat at the same time, as if they'd rehearsed it.

"Good," the woman said.

"Weird," I muttered.

Trevor and Mark peeked around the edge of the door too. I shook my head. The music made my brain feel clogged. I held onto the doorway and watched.

"Stand," the woman said.

Up the kids jumped, like jack-in-the-boxes.

"Shake!" she ordered.

They all held out their right hands and waved them up and down.

"Down lie," she said.

Down lie?

The kids in the room seemed to know what she meant.

They all lay down on the floor!

Whoa! She was training them like dogs!

And they did just what she said—even if she did talk strangely.

Ba-BOOM! Ba-BOOM! went the music. I started to get a headache.

"Stand!" the woman barked, and everybody stood up again. They didn't look right or left. Not a single fidget.

What was wrong with these kids? Why were they being so . . . *good*?

"Speak!" the woman demanded.

"Please!" all the kids cried.

The woman clapped her hands over her ears. "Softer!" she moaned.

"Please," everyone whispered.

"Good, good. Now, what if food I give you?" she

asked. She held out a plate with brown glop on it. "What say you?"

"Thank you!" the kids yelled.

The woman winced. "Softer," she murmured. "Always softer!"

"Thank you," they whispered.

Suddenly Benjy Harrison burped a big loud belch. He clapped his hands over his mouth and glanced around guiltily.

The woman glared at him. "Alert!" she declared.

Immediately, a purple door whooshed open behind her. Three men jogged into the room. They wore pink coveralls with triangle rainbow patches on the shoulders. And they were *huge*. I mean, they looked like pro linebackers.

The woman pointed to Benjy. Benjy blinked and stared at all the other kids in confusion.

The men dashed over to him. Two of them grabbed his arms, while the third seized his legs. They picked him up and carried him out of the room.

"No!" Benjy wailed. "Nooooo!"

The purple door whooshed shut again. None of the kids made a move. They just stared straight ahead. The only sound was the gloppy music with the heavy beat.

I exchanged a horrified glance with Mark.

Where were they taking Benjy?

What were they going to do to him?

Chapter SEVEN

Shaken, I sank back on my heels. I leaned against the wall. Trevor and Mark pulled back too. We stared at one another.

"Do you think we'll ever see Benjy again?" Mark murmured.

"Let's get out of here!" Trevor whispered.

This time I agreed. No way did I want big guys in pink coveralls to show up and drag *us* to who knows where.

We glanced back toward the door that led outside.

Three men in pink coveralls strolled into sight.

We dove behind a trough full of jungle plants.

"Let's find another way out," Trevor whispered.

I peeked around the bottom of the trough. The

guards stood there, staring down the hallway.

My heart thudded. Could they see us?

Trevor tapped my shoulder and pointed to a blue door near our hiding place. I understood what he was thinking. We could get to it without being seen.

"I saw them open one of these," he whispered. "You have to thump something at the edge of the door. There must be some kind of hidden button."

I checked on the guards. They had wandered back down the hall. "Now," I muttered.

Mark and Trevor and I tiptoed over to the door. We thumped around the edge of it.

Mark hit a spot about shoulder high. The door whooshed open, revealing another corridor. It was skinnier and darker than the one we were in, but there were still a lot of plants in it. The air was as hot and wet as a dog's breath.

"Come on!" Trevor urged.

Should we really take a chance? What if there were no other way out?

Stomp, stomp! I heard the guards coming back. No choice!

We jumped over the threshold. Mark tapped the wall again and the door hissed shut.

Several halls branched off from where we stood. "Which way?" I asked.

Trevor bit his lip and pointed to the left.

We wandered through the building for a while. All

the doors were shut, and one hall looked just like another. Twice we had to hide while gigantic guards in pink coveralls tramped by.

I began to get worried. Maybe we made a horrible mistake. Maybe we never should have left the first corridor.

How big could the building be, anyway? Were we getting any closer to a way out?

Or were we heading deeper into the building?

Another patrol approached and we scurried for cover.

I hunched behind a palm tree next to Mark, feeling sweaty and uncomfortable. Trevor squatted beside me, looking worried.

Maybe he was having the same thoughts as I was. Just a little while ago I was desperate to get inside.

Now I might end up spending the rest of my life here!

Mark's stomach gurgled. He clapped his hands over it.

"Did you have to remind me?" I whispered. I was hungry too.

The patrol passed us. We got up to go.

Then Mark tripped on one of the plant pots.

His arms flailed. He staggered, trying to get his balance.

I lunged forward, hoping to catch him before he fell. I strained to reach him—but it was no use.

He fell back against the silver lace on the wall. His head banged a red button.

Whooop! Whooop! Whooop! Alarms started shrieking. Red lights flashed. The floors shook with the tramping of dozens of booted feet.

The guards were on their way.

We were trapped!

Chapter EIGHT

"**S**plit up!" Trevor yelled.

I ran down one corridor. Mark dashed down another. Trevor darted down a third.

I needed to find a hiding place—fast. Otherwise I would run straight into the guards.

I skidded to a stop at a peach-colored door. I banged on the wall with my fist.

Nothing happened.

I banged some more. "Come on, come on," I muttered.

Heavy footsteps thudded behind me. I couldn't waste another second trying to get the stupid door open. I dashed down the corridor.

I glanced back to see how close the guards were.

Whooooooaaaa! My feet flew out from under me. I

must have slipped on a dead leaf.

I rolled over and scrambled behind a big, bushy fern. I scrunched up into a ball and lay there, panting. There wasn't much room. Was I sticking out? I couldn't tell.

A pair of guards hurried down the hall. I could hear them muttering to each other. Their shoes slapped against the slippery carpet.

They were heading right toward me.

I tried to hold as still as possible. But I couldn't stop myself from trembling. The leaves of the big fern shook slightly.

What would they do to me if they caught me?

I mean, this was a place where they taught kids to obey orders. All kinds of kids.

Even I, Valerie Martin, might not be able to resist!

The guards thundered up to where I was hiding.

They stopped right by my fern.

I hunched my shoulders and held on tight to my knees. My heart pounded so loudly, I thought they must be able to hear it. I tried not to breathe.

"Disruptive newbie?" one asked.

"Perhaps. Or intruders in come," the other replied.

"Look-see much?"

"Done sweeps. No scopes."

Huh?

It sounded as if they were speaking English. Kind

of. I could almost understand them, but not quite.

Why did they keep talking? Why didn't they just catch me and get it over with?

The suspense was driving me nuts! I had an incredible urge to stand up and yell, "Here I am!"

Luckily, I didn't. A minute later, the guards moved on.

A few seconds after that, the alarm switched off.

I waited and listened to the quiet for a long time. I worried about Mark and Trevor. Did they get caught? Were they okay? Where were they?

Where was I? Could I find my way out?

I checked my watch. Almost four-thirty. I stood up slowly and glanced up and down the halls. All clear.

I headed back the way I came, checking around every bend before I rounded it. Lots of plants, no more patrols.

But which way was out?

"Pssst!"

I whirled around at the sound. It seemed to come from a big dark leafy plant. I held my breath and studied it.

Trevor peeked out through the leaves.

"Phew!" I blew out my breath. "You're all right! I thought you guys got caught."

"We hid," Mark whispered. "I found Trevor about ten minutes ago. We didn't know where you were. We were trying to figure out how to find you."

"*Come on*," Trevor urged. "Let's get out of here!"

He led us to a dark blue door. We thumped the wall around it. The door whooshed open. Cool dry air rushed in.

We rushed outside. Sky! Other buildings! A car driving past! It was all so *normal*.

I noticed that this wasn't the same door we went in. No guard station next to it, for one thing. For another, we came out on Poplar Drive instead of Oak Street.

We must have gone right through the building and come out the back. I was kind of surprised it was only a block long. It felt as if we'd walked for miles inside.

Mark glanced over his shoulder at the big blue building. "They might come out looking for us. Let's get away," he said nervously.

"Yeah. Far away," Trevor agreed.

"Meeting," I announced. "My house."

Mark and Trevor and I ran to my house. We snagged sodas and I grabbed a super-size bag of potato chips. Then we hurried down to the rec room in the basement.

"Okay," I began when we were sitting with the chips open in front of us. "What is going on in that building?"

"They sure aren't playing chess," Mark declared.

"They make machines that do weird things," I

observed. I studied my hand again, the one that had been wrapped by that silver glove. It seemed okay now.

"They like plants and hot weather," Mark stated.

"They have a lot of guards," Trevor added.

"They make kids obey orders," Mark said with a shiver.

"Yeah. The big question is—why?" I stared down at my soda can, then glanced up at Trevor and Mark. "I think we need to go back there."

"Do we have to?" Mark groaned. "That place is scary!"

"Yeah. Totally scary," Trevor agreed. "I think we should just forget about it."

I shook my head. What kind of attitude was that?

If the investigators on *Strange Cases* quit every time they found something scary, the show would be off the air!

"Scary means it's important," I argued. "You saw what they were doing—and to kids we know. We need to find out more."

Mark glared at me through his glasses. Trevor chewed on his lower lip.

"You know I'm right," I added. I stared at Mark.

Finally, he nodded reluctantly. I glanced at Trevor. "What about you? Are you in?" I demanded.

Trevor nodded. Slowly.

"Okay," I told him. "Let's keep it between us three."

"No problem," Trevor promised. "I won't say a word."

"Tomorrow let's ask kids about the clubs," I suggested.

"Agreed," Mark said. But he didn't sound very enthusiastic.

Friday morning, one of the first people I saw at school was Benjy Harrison. He stood by his locker. He didn't look any different. Whatever those guards did to him when they carried him away must not have been too bad.

Usually I keep my distance from Benjy. He's kind of a bully. He has particular kids he likes to pick on, but I'm not one of them. I try to keep it that way.

But today I walked right up to him.

"Are you okay?" I asked.

"Huh?" He glared down at me.

"Do you feel okay?" I yelled. I yell when I get nervous.

His mouth twisted into a frown. "I'm fine. Why?"

"I—um—I wondered if you like that Two Ts Club you're in."

"Sure I like it," he replied. The suspicious look faded from his eyes. "I *love* it!"

I thought about getting out my notebook, like the guys on *Strange Cases*. But I decided Benjy might think that was weird.

"What kind of club is it, anyway?" I asked.

Benjy blinked a few times. "It's—a video game club." He smiled. "We go to a room where they have these great video games, and we play all afternoon. We don't even have to pay."

What? A video game club?

That wasn't what *I* saw. Not even close.

"They have all the newest games!" Benjy declared. His eyes lit up. "Ones with really big explosions! And you can beat up other guys with kung fu! I *love* that club!"

"Is that what you did yesterday?" I asked.

Benjy nodded enthusiastically.

I didn't know what to think. Was he lying to me? Was this some kind of joke?

He seemed so sincere.

Did those guards who carried him away take him to a video game room?

And why didn't he say anything about the dog-training part of the afternoon? Why didn't Elaine mention that part either?

Stand! Sit! Shake! How could they forget that?

I studied Benjy. He seemed to be in some kind of weird trance. He made gunfire and explosion sound effects, like he was reliving a great video game session. "Blam! Up in smoke!" he yelled.

"Just like your brain," I muttered.

That's when it hit me.

Could that be the answer?

Yes. It had to be.

It was horrible. But it explained the way he was acting.

Benjy had been brainwashed!

Chapter NINE

Brainwashing! That must be what was happening to the kids in the after-school clubs.

I had to talk to Mark and Trevor!

The bell rang and I rushed to class. I planned to talk to them in the few seconds while everyone was settling down.

But when I hurried into my classroom, all the kids were already in their seats. They sat staring silently at Mr. Hool. Everyone but Mark and Trevor had their books out and their hands folded.

Whoa! Total politeness.

Mr. Hool smiled his creepy smile. "Good morning, children," he murmured. "Please pass your 'good manners' essays to the front of the room. Winners will be announced next Monday."

I slid into my seat and yanked out my notebook. I'd managed to write only two paragraphs. I peeked over at Mark.

He was handing in three whole pages!

I guess he really wanted to go to Neverland.

I didn't get a chance to talk to Mark and Trevor until lunch. We found a table in the back of the room, by the wall.

I decided it might be better to prepare Mark and Trevor for my theory before I sprang it on them. So I nudged Mark. "Check out the kids in our class."

He and Trevor glanced around the room.

"Wow," Mark commented.

"Wow what?" Trevor asked, frowning.

"The Two Ts kids and the M-W kids are sitting in separate groups," I explained.

"Don't they usually split up like that?" Trevor asked.

"No way!" Mark scoffed.

"Trevor doesn't know this stuff. He's new," I reminded Mark. I turned to Trevor. "Normally David Lubin wouldn't be caught anywhere near Benjy," I explained. "And Elaine always sits with Alison. They're best friends. Now they're at different tables."

"And look how they're acting," Mark added. "So . . . *good*."

He was right. All around, kids from other grades

and classes yelled, blew bubbles in their milk, threw napkins, grabbed food off each other's trays. The usual.

But not the kids in *our* class. They were using forks and knives. Taking small bites. Conversing politely.

They were *not* normal sixth graders.

"Did you guys find out anything new?" Trevor asked.

"I asked four different people what kind of club they go to." Mark got out a little notebook. "Here's what they said: A model-building club. A card collector's club. A club for people who want to draw superheroes. A tea-party club. Everybody says it's just the kind of club they always wanted to join."

"Benjy claims it's a video game club," I reported. "And I asked Elaine again when I gave her back her key card. She still insists it's a chess club." I turned to Trevor. "What about you?"

"I heard it's a club for magicians," he replied.

"And none of them said *anything* about being trained to sit!" Mark declared. "So what gives?"

Time to tell them my theory. I took a deep breath.

"I think these kids are being brainwashed," I stated.

Mark and Trevor stared at me.

"Are you serious?" Trevor demanded.

"She's serious," Mark confirmed, still staring at me.

"We better talk about this later," I said. "In the meantime, keep asking about the clubs. Hey, Trevor, let me have your phone number in case I need to call you."

Trevor bit his lip. "Okay, but my parents are really strict about phone time. I can get phone calls only up until five-thirty in the afternoon."

"Wow. Harsh!" I commented.

"Yeah," he muttered.

I glanced around the table. "So let's meet at my house again right after school."

"Are we still going to the movies?" Mark asked.

"Huh?" Trevor said.

"Val and I were going to the movies tonight. Wanna come?" Mark tore into a packet of Twinkies.

"Oh, yeah," I murmured. Mark and I had been talking about going to see *Destructor*, the new Hans Heller movie, for weeks. Hans Heller is our favorite action-movie actor.

Destructor opened tonight. And I almost forgot about it! Unbelievable!

I must be really worried.

After supper Friday night, Trevor, Mark, and I went to the movies. *Destructor* was playing at the Shadyside Movie Palace, which had just been rebuilt. The place looked awesome! It was the first theater I'd ever been in with a balcony. All the other movie theaters I'd been to were part of multiplexes, with puny little screens.

Mark, Trevor, and I got a tub of popcorn to split and some sodas. We headed for the balcony. Everyone else had the same idea, so it was crowded. But we snagged seats near the front.

I gazed around. "Hey, notice something strange?" I asked.

"Those Greek temple murals on the wall?" Mark replied.

I shook my head. "No one from our class is here."

Mark's eyes swept the balcony. Then he leaned over the rail and peered down. "You're right. How could they miss the new Hans Heller movie?"

"Maybe they're so *good* now they're spending Friday nights doing homework." I shuddered. I never wanted to be *that* good.

"Shhh," Trevor whispered as the lights went down. "The movie's starting."

I gazed up at the screen. It was huge! I felt as if I were right in the middle of it.

About halfway through the movie, the bad guys were closing in on Hans Heller and the beautiful government agent.

"I have to go to the bathroom," Mark muttered. He stood up and headed for the lobby.

I knew he didn't really have to go. The truth is, he gets so wrapped up in Hans Heller movies he can't *stand* the really tense parts. He always ducks out.

Hans and the beautiful government agent were trapped on the top floor of a burning building. There was only one way out. They had to jump across to another building.

Hans went first, then turned back to catch the beautiful agent. "Chump! You can do it!" Hans yelled to her. "Chump!"

I blinked a couple of times. My head began to ache.

The next thing I knew, people in the theater were screaming and yelling. And pointing.

Only they weren't pointing at the screen.

They were pointing at *me*!

I stared down at them. And figured out why they were screaming.

I was teetering on the balcony railing.

And I really wanted to jump!

Chapter TEN

Below me, a sea of faces stared up, screaming, pointing.

How did I get up here?

What was I doing?

Oh, no! My feet! They were slipping!

I pinwheeled my arms, desperately trying to fall backwards instead of forwards. My heart pounded. Blood drummed in my ears.

"Noooo!" I screamed.

I was falling!

Then someone grabbed me around the waist. Whoever it was yanked me away from the edge. I stared up into pale blue eyes.

Trevor!

My legs wouldn't support me. I threw my arms

around his neck. I clung to him, terrified.

Trevor backed up the stairs to our seats, tugging me along. My toes dragged on the carpet. "Cut it out," he muttered, trying to pull my arms from around him. He glanced around.

I realized other kids were watching us.

Watching me hang on to geeky Trevor Dean!

Oh, ultimate groan!

What if they told the kids in my class? I'd never hear the end of it.

But I didn't want to let go. I was still scared and shaky. I could still see all those faces staring up at me. Wondering if I was going to jump. And me wanting to!

"Valerie!" Trevor whispered, pushing me away from him.

I let go of him and slumped into my seat. I gripped the chair arms so hard, my hands hurt.

"What happened?" he asked.

"I'm not sure," I muttered.

But I had an idea. A very scary idea.

Hans Heller ordered the woman on the screen to jump.

Ordered! Just like the training lady in the blue building. "Sit! Stand! Shake!"

Jump!

Those kids in the clubs were brainwashed to obey orders.

What if somehow *I* got brainwashed too?

The movie stuttered to a stop and the houselights came up. An usher approached. "You two. Come with me!" he said.

Trevor and I followed him out to the lobby. I hung on to the railing the whole flight down.

"What was all that commotion?" the usher demanded when we reached the lobby.

Mark, who was standing by the candy counter, noticed us. He rushed over. "What's going on?"

The usher ignored him. "Don't you know that what you did is very dangerous? You could have been hurt!"

"I didn't mean to do it," I whispered, shaken.

Mark's eyes widened. "What happened?" he asked.

"Tell you later," Trevor whispered.

"You'd better promise not to do anything like that again," the usher warned me, "or we'll bar you from the movie house."

"I—" I began. I shivered.

How could I be sure I wouldn't do anything like that again? What if some other movie character ordered me to do something? How could I stop myself from obeying?

I felt sick to my stomach. I glanced at Mark and Trevor. "Can we go home?" I asked in a small voice. "We have to talk."

*   *   *

Mom and Dad were surprised when we came home so early.

"The movie was no good?" Dad asked.

I didn't want to tell them what happened. No way could I explain. So I just shrugged.

"It was lame," I replied. "We're going downstairs, okay?"

I followed Mark and Trevor to the basement. I was still shivering, so I grabbed a comforter from the closet. I wrapped myself up in it before I sat down.

I never knew being terrified could make a person so cold!

"Okay, Val. What happened?" Mark demanded.

"Hans Heller ordered the beautiful government agent to jump," I began. "And I tried to jump. Right off the balcony!"

"Oh, no!" Mark gasped.

I stared at my hands. "You know what this means, don't you?"

Trevor and Mark were silent.

I took a deep breath. "I've been brainwashed too."

I shuddered. Saying it out loud made me feel even worse.

We sat there for a minute. Finally Mark said slowly, "So if I yell 'Stand!' . . ."

All three of us shot to our feet.

We stared at each other, eyes wide.

"Sit!" I ordered.

WHOMP! We all sat with a thump on the couch. Dust billowed up around us from the couch cushions.

"Shake!" Trevor commanded.

Our right hands came up in front of us. We pumped them up and down. Just like the kids we'd seen in the blue building.

"Stand!" Mark called.

"Shake!" I shouted.

"Sit!" Trevor cried.

We went up and down as if we were on springs.

"Jump!" I ordered.

We scrambled to our feet and jumped in the air.

I couldn't believe it! We looked like jumping jacks.

Mark started laughing. Then Trevor started laughing.

"It isn't funny!" I yelled.

"Oh, yeah? Shake!" Mark commanded.

All our hands worked at the same time.

I started to giggle. It *was* funny. In a creepy way.

"I wonder if there's a way to get us to shiver when I say 'shake,'" Mark muttered.

"Hey. You just said shake and we didn't do it," I noted.

"Maybe it has to be a command," Trevor reasoned. "Or a special tone of voice."

"So I could say 'we shake the milk shakes,' and—" Mark's eyes darted back and forth between our hands.

None of us reached out for a handshake that time.

Then I thought of something. "How come when Hans said 'jump' you didn't jump?" I asked Trevor. "Why was I the only one?"

Trevor turned pink. "I didn't know he was saying 'jump,'" he explained. "He has a weird accent. I thought he said 'chump.' I thought he was calling that agent lady names."

I rolled my eyes. "Where have *you* been?" I didn't even notice Hans Heller's accent anymore.

I leaned forward. "So how did this happen to us?" I asked. "We didn't join either of those clubs."

"Hey." Mark frowned. "Remember at lunch, how we planned to meet here after school?"

"Yeah," I replied impatiently. "So?"

"So . . ." Mark scratched his head. "*Did* we meet?"

"Did we—" I began. Then I stopped.

I couldn't remember! I glanced at Trevor.

"I don't—" Trevor shook his head. "I think—"

"My mind is a complete blank," I gasped.

"I don't remember anything between leaving school around three and my mom calling me to supper." Mark shuddered.

"I can't remember what happened after I left school either," I murmured. "Not until I set the table for dinner."

"Wait. I don't get it," Trevor said. "Two Ts. M-W. There is no club on Fridays."

"Or ... is there?" I grabbed my wallet from my back pocket and peered inside.

A sliver of white gleamed from the pocket for dollar bills. I gripped it and pulled out—a key card!

I knew I gave Elaine's back to her at recess that morning. What was I doing with a card?

Mark got his wallet out and checked through it.

"I have one too," he whispered.

We stared at Trevor. He licked his lips, then pulled out his wallet and looked inside. He, too, held up a key card.

I swallowed hard.

It looked as if Mark, Trevor, and I had joined a club after all.

Chapter ELEVEN

"**B**ut *how*?" Mark demanded. "How did we join?"

I frowned. "I wonder if Mr. Hool did something to us. I mean, the clubs are his idea. He must be in on this brainwashing thing, right?"

"Mr. Hool?" Mark echoed. He and Trevor stared at me as if I said something rude. "But he's so nice!"

"Yeah," I muttered. "As nice as all the brainwashed kids are now." But I didn't push it. I didn't feel up to arguing.

Trevor and Mark didn't stay much longer. I think we were all too freaked out to keep talking.

After they left, I went up and sat on the edge of my bed. Thinking.

I remembered how I felt as I perched on that balcony railing. If it weren't for Trevor, I would have fallen for sure.

Could I ever watch a movie again?

What if people on TV shows ordered each other around?

What if they used some of the special training words?

What if Mom or Dad did? What if my little sister, Amy, did?

I couldn't live like this!

I brushed my teeth and washed my face. I heard Amy in the hall. To be safe, I waited until I heard her door close before I left the bathroom.

Then I went straight to bed.

I lay in the dark, staring up at nothing.

But no matter how much I thought and thought, I couldn't figure this out by myself.

At last I decided I had to tell Mom and Dad what was going on. Maybe they could do some grown up thing that would solve this problem.

I hoped.

Saturday morning I woke up early and hurried downstairs. I wanted to talk to Mom and Dad right away.

Dad was making scrambled eggs with paprika and sliced black olives and pepperoni. He cooks breakfast most Saturdays—usually eggs with weird things in them. I just eat whatever he makes and try not to think about it.

Amy sat reading a fat book. As usual.

Mom sipped coffee. She glanced up when I came in and smiled at me. "Morning."

"Morning. I—I have something to tell you," I declared.

"This sounds serious." Mom put down her coffee mug, and Dad set down his spatula.

"It's about this club," I began.

"Yes?"

"This club I joined." I was having trouble starting.

"A club? I thought you didn't like clubs, Valerie," Mom remarked. "What kind of club is it?"

"They—" I meant to say: *They brainwashed me! They make me follow orders!*

Instead, what came out was, "It's a chess club. It's great! I love it!"

Huh? Where did that come from? That wasn't what I planned to say. The words just popped out.

Then I found myself speaking again.

"It's the kind of club I've wanted to join all my life!" I gushed.

Just the way Benjy gushed when I asked him about the club.

I could feel my mouth smiling. I tried to stop, but I couldn't. My face muscles wouldn't obey me.

Let me try this one more time, I thought. Don't panic.

"I mean—" I began again. *They hypnotized me! I didn't even know I joined the club! Something terrible is happening!*

Those were the words in my brain. But I couldn't get them to come out of my mouth.

My throat just closed up. I sat there with my mouth open like an idiot.

"Yes, honey?" Dad asked.

My mouth moved as if it belonged to someone else. "I'm just so *happy!*"

"I'm glad." Dad smiled. "I always hoped you'd find some other chess players your own age."

But I didn't! I tried to explain.

"It's perfect!" was what I said.

The fight between my brain and my mouth was giving me a headache. And my mouth was definitely winning.

It was so frustrating. I could feel my face turning red.

I, Valerie Martin, had plans for the rest of my life.

Now it seemed as if somebody else did too.

And that *somebody* was in control.

Chapter TWELVE

"**Y**our club is perfect? You're happy? That's what you wanted to tell us?" Mom asked.

"No, I—there's this—yes, that's all."

I didn't even sound like me. My voice was kind of stretched out. And really prissy.

I fought to say something else, but my throat closed up completely. I felt as if I were strangling!

Finally I gave up. I stared at my place mat.

As soon as I stopped trying to talk, my throat relaxed.

"Have some eggs," Dad offered, scooping this week's egg surprise onto a plate for me.

"Thank you," I replied politely.

I didn't know what else to do, and I was hungry, so I ate breakfast. It was probably gross. Dad could have made scrambled eggs with fried worms and I wouldn't have noticed.

Every time I thought about someone else controlling what I could say and do, I shook with terror. What was going on in Shadyside?

Why would someone want to control sixth graders? Why would someone want to turn us all into sixth-grade zombies?

After breakfast I called Mark. "I tried to tell Mom and Dad about the brainwashing," I told him.

"You *did*?" He sounded shocked. But hopeful. "So what happened?"

"It was horrible! I tried to explain, but instead I started babbling about what a wonderful club it was. It was like I couldn't control my own mouth. I'd think one thing—but then other words would come out."

Total silence on the other end of the phone.

I waited a minute, then asked, "Are you there?"

"Still here. Wow. But you can talk to me about it."

He was right. "Yeah. I guess."

"Probably because we're both in it. It doesn't matter what you tell me, because I already know."

I shuddered. "This is *sooo* creepy."

"I'm going to try to tell *my* parents," Mark announced. "I'll talk to you later." He hung up.

I waited awhile, but he didn't call back.

I stayed close to my room for the rest of the

weekend. I wasn't taking any chances. I was afraid to leave the house.

What if someone told me to go jump in Fear Lake? It *could* happen!

Monday morning I decided I had to go to school. No way would Mom and Dad let me stay home unless I was really sick. And they're hard to fool.

Besides, I couldn't spend the rest of my life in my room. I wasn't feeling much like being a secret government agent these days. But I knew one thing: I had to find out what those people in the blue building did to us.

And then I had to figure out how to undo it.

In class, everyone was dying for Mr. Hool to announce the winners of the essay contest. Everyone but me. I already knew there was no way I won.

So instead I studied Mr. Hool as he talked.

"The ten winners will have an all-expense-paid week in Neverland, including meals and hotel," he declared.

I stared at him with narrowed eyes. He was big— like all the people in the weird blue building. But he didn't talk strangely, like they did. And his clothes were normal. No pink coverall.

Was he one of them? I couldn't tell.

"Get your parents to sign these permission slips

tonight," he instructed. He waved pink slips of paper. "And pack clothes for a week. Bring your things when you come to school tomorrow! You'll leave right after school. I'll be going along with the winners as a chaperon. I'm sure the rest of you will behave for the substitute."

Total silence in the classroom. Everyone stared at Mr. Hool, waiting for him to announce the winners.

Finally he began to read the names of the ten lucky kids.

"Mark Meyers," he called.

Whoa! Mark won!

"Oh, boy, oh, boy!" he yelled. "A week in Neverland! Yes!"

I smiled at him and tried not to feel jealous.

Mr. Hool winced and glared at Mark. "Quiet!" he snapped.

Mark's mouth snapped shut. Just like that.

He rolled his eyes, frantic.

Quiet must be one of the commands we were taught.

Did Mr. Hool know that? Or was it just an accident? I couldn't decide.

Mark began to make gagging sounds. His throat must be closing up. I knew how he felt.

"Calm down," I tried to whisper.

Nothing came out. *Quiet* worked on me too.

We *had* to get rid of this training!

*   *   *

"So did you try to tell your parents about the club?" I asked Mark at lunch. By then we could both speak again.

I wasn't sure where Trevor was. But I was relieved that none of the other kids in our class had heard about what happened at the movie theater. Especially the part where I grabbed on to him.

"Yeah," Mark replied. "But the same thing happened to me. I couldn't say anything but totally dumb stuff." He frowned. "I kept telling them it was a nature club. "We're studying plants! I'm so happy!' It was awful!"

I shook my head. "We have to do something. And fast."

After school Mark and I followed the M-W kids to the big, blue building. We stayed a few steps behind them.

We had gone only about half a block when Trevor joined us. He looked even geekier than usual today. I swear his pants were two inches above his ankles. "What's up?" he asked. "What are you doing?"

"We're going back to the clubhouse," I told him.

"We have to find some way to unwash our brains," Mark added.

Trevor's pale face grew paler. But then he nodded. "Right." He began walking alongside us.

Normally I'd tell him that Mark and I were our own

team. But Trevor seemed smart. And I had a feeling we were going to need all the help we could get.

We got out our key cards and filed through the front door a few steps behind the other kids. The hot, wet air wrapped around me like a damp sheet. I started sweating right away.

The M-W Club members headed straight for the room where we saw the other kids being trained.

Trevor, Mark, and I hid behind a bush down the hall. The syrupy music with the heavy bass thudded through the floor to where we were.

"It won't do us any good to go into the training room," Mark whispered. "Unless maybe we could tape that sappy music and play it backwards."

"Play the music backwards?" I stared at him. "Why?"

Mark adjusted his glasses. "I read an article about brainwashing over the weekend. It said music is often used as part of the brainwashing."

"And playing it backwards will reverse the brainwashing? Did you bring a tape recorder?" I asked excitedly.

Mark shook his head. "I don't think playing it backwards really works," he told me. "It's just a myth."

"Anyway, if we go in there, we'll just get caught," Trevor pointed out.

I didn't have a clue about what to do. But I knew standing around wasn't helping.

We had to do *something*!

"Let's look in there." I pointed to a peach-colored door.

We checked the hall for patrols, then approached the door. We started thumping the door frame about chest high. I hit the right spot and the door whooshed open. I peeked in.

No people.

We darted inside. Seconds later the door whooshed shut.

In the middle of the room stood a clear tube about six feet tall and three feet across. It had an oval opening on the side.

A post sprouted from the floor next to the tube. A flat control pad covered with buttons perched on top of it.

I went over and tapped the tube. "Wonder what this does."

It didn't feel like glass or plastic. More like metal.

Metal you could see through?

Mark headed for the control pad. "Maybe if you get inside that tube, it can fix your brain."

"Or totally erase it," Trevor suggested gloomily. "I don't think we should touch it."

"There's no way to tell what it does unless we experiment," I pointed out. I felt a little sick to my stomach.

This could be a big mistake.

"Nobody's in it now. Let's see what happens when I push this big green button." Mark reached toward the control pad.

"No!" Trevor yelled, just as Mark punched the button.

A high-pitched hum filled the room.

The air in the tube sparkled with tiny glints of light.

The lights grew brighter until it hurt to look at them. The humming swelled.

Suddenly a chord of music chimed—like when a computer boots up, only super-loud. The sparks in the tube vanished.

A shadow darkened in the center of the tube. Colors shone across its outside edges.

The shadow grew thicker. The colors brightened.

We stared with our mouths open.

Finally the shadow took on a shape.

A recognizable shape.

There was a human being in that tube.

Chapter THIRTEEN

A tall, white-haired woman in a shiny dark green coverall glared at us from inside the tube.

She reached for the oval door.

Mark grabbed my arm. "Come on!"

"Let's get out of here!" Trevor cried.

All three of us dashed for the door. Trevor tapped the dark spot on the frame. The door whooshed open and we raced through.

"Run!" Trevor screamed.

I ran with Mark beside me. Trevor followed on our heels. Alarms screeched before we got very far down the hall.

"We can't go out the front," Trevor gasped between quick breaths. "The guard will catch us. This way!"

He led us through the skinnier, darker corridors toward the back of the building.

"There it is!" Mark cried at last.

The back door!

Whooooosh!

Out we tumbled. The cool, fresh air tasted awesome.

"We better keep going," I panted.

"Okay," Trevor agreed.

We ran down the block. I didn't think I could run any farther without a rest. I spotted the bowling alley.

"Let's go inside," I gasped.

We ran in and stopped at the snack bar. I treated everybody to sodas. We carried them to a table far from the counter and sat down.

"What happened in there?" Mark asked. His face was pale with fear. I figured mine was too.

I leaned forward. "It looked like a transporter from *Star Trek*."

"Nobody has machines like that!" Mark objected. "Maybe that lady was just a hologram or something."

"Duhhh! She stared right at us!" I snapped.

"Holograms can do that."

"What if she *was* real? What if she was transported in from someplace else? Who are those people?" The words tumbled out of me as I grew more upset. "Maybe they're aliens! Horrible aliens who want to rule our planet, starting with sixth graders!"

"Hold on. Has anybody been hurt because of this brainwashing stuff?" Trevor asked.

"How about almost jumping off a balcony!" I shot back.

Trevor stared at the table and moodily sipped his soda.

"And why can't we talk to a grown up about it?" I asked. "When I tried to tell my parents on Saturday, all these words came out of my mouth that I didn't even think up!"

"The same thing happened to me," Mark added.

Trevor stared at us both. "I never tried," he admitted.

"Don't bother," I told him. "It won't work. We're on our own."

We thought about that for a minute. A long, scary minute.

"What do we do next?" Mark asked. His voice shook a little. "I want my own brain back!" His wide eyes darted from me to Trevor. Trevor gazed at him and shuddered.

I tore a napkin to shreds. "I don't know. I just don't know." I sighed and rubbed my face. "We'll figure it out tomorrow. If I think anymore today, my brain will explode."

Mark pulled a pink permission slip out of his pocket. "Tomorrow . . ."

I almost forgot. Tomorrow Mark would be on his way to Neverland.

And Trevor and I would be on our own. Still brainwashed.

Tuesday I rode my bike to school. Mark wouldn't be walking home or anywhere else with me for a week. I wasn't looking forward to his going away.

After school, Trevor and I watched Mark, the other nine contest winners, and Mr. Hool climb on the bus that would take them to Neverland.

It wasn't a regular school bus—more like a super van. It looked cool. I wished I were on it with Mark instead of stuck in Shadyside with a scary problem I didn't know how to solve.

"Lucky Mark," I muttered.

"What's so great about Neverland?" Trevor asked, frowning.

"Haven't you ever been there?"

He shrugged. "No."

"How could you not go to Neverland?" I exclaimed. "It's the most awesome place!"

"I just moved here, remember?"

"Oh, right. Neverland has the best rides in the world. Super slides, logjams, roller coasters that do complete loops! And this one ride, I know Mark will go on it. It's our absolute favorite ride at Neverland."

"What does it do?" Trevor asked.

"It's called the Deathwatch. You ride in a little car up a long, long clanking spiral. At the top there are these animatronic vultures. The cars slow down while you go past them. They clack their beaks and say, 'Tasty morsels! Prepare to meet your doom! Yum! Yum! Jump right down and DIE!' Then the cars swoop waaaaaaay down, shimmying and shaking all the way to the bottom. It's a six-screamer! I love it—"

Then it hit me.

"Jump!" I cried.

I bounced into the air. Trevor gave a little hop too. "Don't do that," he snapped, shooting me an irritated look.

But I barely even noticed. "Oh, no," I groaned. "Oh, no!"

I could picture it. Mark would go on Deathwatch. And then, on top of the highest loop, the vultures would order him to jump.

And he would!

"I've got to stop him," I muttered.

"Stop who?" Trevor stared at me.

"No time to explain." I leaped onto my bike and pedaled as hard as I could after the bus, leaving Trevor behind.

I had to catch up before they left town.

I had to warn Mark not to ride Deathwatch.

I pedaled as hard as I had ever pedaled in my life. Breath screamed in and out of my lungs.

There! Up ahead of me! I spotted the bus.

It turned left on Oak Street—and stopped in front of the ice-blue building.

I pulled up behind a bush across the street and hopped off my bike.

Mr. Hool stepped down from the bus and stood watching.

All the kids filed off the bus, Mark in the lead.

Mr. Hool nodded to the guard. The door slid open.

So he *was* one of them. I was right about him.

And now he had Mark!

I didn't stop to think. I waited about two seconds. Then I used my key card to follow them.

The hot, wet air hit me in the face. I glimpsed Mr. Hool's sweatered figure vanishing around a corner.

I shadowed the group along the corridors. They stopped in front of a peach-colored door. Mr. Hool tapped the wall. The door whooshed open.

I knew what was inside that room. The glass tube! Would Mark recognize the room and wake up?

Please, oh, please, oh, please!

I crept from my hiding place and ran to the doorway.

Just in time to see Mark step into the tube.

Mr. Hool stood in front of the control pad. I saw

his thumb lowering over the big green button.

No.

He pressed it.

No!

The high-pitched humming sounded all through the room, and the air in the tube sparkled. The music swelled and chimed. Blank-faced, Mark just stood there for a few seconds.

Then he vanished.

Chapter FOURTEEN

"**N**o!" I screamed.

I couldn't help it.

My best friend just disappeared into nowhere! Right in front of me. Vanished!

I couldn't stop screaming.

Mr. Hool whirled around. He towered over me, glaring at me with his magnified-because-of-glasses eyes. "Quiet!" he ordered.

The screams stopped coming out of my mouth. But I could still hear them in my head.

Mark! Where was Mark? What did they do to him?

"Stay!" Mr. Hool said.

I finally figured out I should run away. But now I couldn't move.

Mr. Hool marched over to a wall and punched a

button. All the other contest winners stood totally still, not even glancing around. "Alert!" Mr. Hool barked at the wall.

Patrol guys in pink coveralls showed up in seconds.

One of them slipped headphones over my head.

I heard that sickly sweet music, the kind I first heard in the training room. My head started to throb.

And then I began to feel sleepy. . . .

I folded napkins in half and placed them on the place mats. I laid forks on top of them, carefully, so everything lined up.

Then I stood back and gazed at the table. Perfect!

Well, almost perfect. I moved a cup half an inch.

That did it!

Mom hurried through the dining room. "I think Mark left these here a while ago," she told me, holding up some wool gloves.

Mark. I hoped he was okay.

Wait. Why wouldn't he be? He was on a trip to Neverland! He was probably at the Pirate's Tavern, the coolest restaurant in Neverland, eating dinner with the other essay-winners.

Right?

A horrible feeling sneaked through me.

I blinked. *Forget it*, I thought.

I went to the kitchen, where Mom was checking the oven.

"Can I help you with anything?" I asked.

Mom shut the oven door and stood up. "What did you say?"

"Can I help you with anything?" I repeated.

Being helpful is good.

"If you want an advance on your allowance, Val, the answer is no." Mom bustled over to the refrigerator.

"I don't need an advance."

Mom stared at me with narrowed eyes for a second, then handed me a head of lettuce. "Okay. Make the salad."

I tore at the lettuce leaves, trying to break them into even bite-sized pieces. Mark, I thought. Neverland. Mark.

Why couldn't I stop worrying about him?

I had to call Trevor. Maybe he'd know why I was so worried.

I dialed the number he gave me. Then I noticed the time. It was almost six. I was supposed to call Trevor only until 5:30.

Oh, well. What could they do, shoot me?

Not over the phone!

"Greetings," a woman's voice said. "Yes? How help you I may?"

Her voice sounded familiar. So did her weird way of talking.

"Is Trevor there?" I asked.

"Trevor? Who this is?" she snapped.

And then I knew where I'd heard that voice before.

She was the kid-training lady from the clubhouse! The one who said, "Sit! Stand! Shake! Down lie!"

Chapter FIFTEEN

I slammed the phone down.

My mind whirled, trying to piece it all together.

Trevor's phone . . . the training lady . . . the clubhouse . . .

The clubhouse!

Mark!

I suddenly remembered chasing the bus on my bike. Right! I had to warn Mark about the Deathwatch ride at Neverland.

But Mark never made it to Neverland.

He stepped into that big glass tube and disappeared.

And then Mr. Hool caught me and made me forget.

But I remembered now. I must be so worried that my fear broke through the training.

I *had* to get to the clubhouse and find Mark!

"Who was that?" Mom asked, staring at me and the phone.

I jumped. "Must have been a wrong number," I answered.

But I knew it wasn't. It was the number Trevor gave me. And the training woman was there!

Did they have Trevor, too? Did they put him in that tube and send him to who knows where?

Maybe I should go to his house and make sure he was okay.

But I had no idea where he lived.

Anyway, I had to find Mark. Right away.

"Gotta go," I told Mom.

"Valerie, it's supper time. You can't go out now."

For a second I couldn't think. "Uh—I have to go— uh—wash my hands," I said at last.

"You've been making salad with dirty hands?" Mom took the lettuce to the sink and began washing it. She looked mad.

I headed for the front bathroom, then darted right past it and out the front door. There was no point in trying to explain anything to Mom. Even if I could get the words out, she would never believe me.

My bike wasn't locked up in the garage, where it belonged. It must still be in front of the blue building.

I ran all the way.

The light was off in the guard station, and no one watched from behind the glass. I tried my key card in the yellow door.

Whoosh! The door opened. I stepped into that swampy air.

The ceiling panels seemed dimmer, as though even in this windowless hall it was night.

I headed straight to the room with the glass tube in it. I knocked on the door frame.

The door hissed open.

The tube gleamed in the silver light.

I went straight to the control panel. I stared at the big green button Mark pushed to make the lady appear. The one Mr. Hool pushed to make Mark disappear.

Other multicolored buttons crowded the panel like rows of kernels on a corncob. No labels!

What did all this stuff do?

I glanced into the tube. Maybe there were labels inside.

The round floor in the tube was paved with pebbles of peach-colored light. I noticed colored spots stenciled against one wall of the tube and climbed in to get a better look at them.

A little section of glass was stained with colored squares and dots. I leaned closer. The biggest square was green, like the big button on the console. Floating buttons?

If you wanted to operate the tube and you were the only one around, it made sense to have buttons on the inside, I figured.

The room's door whooshed open.

My head whipped around.

It was the training lady!

And she saw me!

"What do you here?" she asked.

All I needed was for her to tell me to "stay" and put those headphones over my head again. I'd forget everything.

No way. Not twice in one day.

I jabbed my thumb on the green spot of glass.

The air filled with sparks. The floor hummed.

My stomach lurched. I shut my eyes tight. I felt as if I were falling in a dream.

Then the fizzing sparkles popped and faded, and the humming lowered until it disappeared.

Time to open my eyes.

But I was afraid.

What would I see?

Chapter SIXTEEN

I took a deep breath and opened my eyes.

Hey! The room looked exactly the same.

Except the lady in the pink coverall was gone.

I stepped out of the tube.

Same gray walls and floor, with all that lacy silver stuff across it. Same hot wet air. Same control panel on a post.

I listened at the door. I couldn't hear anything— no alarms, no footsteps, no conversation.

The coast was clear.

I tapped the door frame and the door slid out of the way.

I gazed out at a dark green hallway. The stiff brown carpet was gone. Now moss sprouted on the floor. Long, twisting vines grew up the walls and across the light-covered ceiling. I heard water running somewhere nearby.

I had never seen *this* place before!

I glanced over my shoulder at the glass tube.

Should I climb back in and press the green button?

Or would it send me right back to the training lady?

Or somewhere else besides home?

Could Mark be here somehow?

I stepped nervously into the green hall. The door shut behind me. I turned to take a good look at it. I wanted to be able to find that door again.

It was still peach-colored. I would have marked it, but I didn't have a pen.

An air current blew from the left-hand corridor. I headed that way, hoping I'd find a door to the outside.

The mossy corridor opened out into a bigger one almost immediately. This one had fewer plants, and lots more silver lace on the upper walls.

It also had people.

I went around a bend and nearly ran smack into a group of men and women. They all wore shiny coveralls—some red, some blue, some green.

My heart nearly stopped. I was trapped! No way could I hide from these people!

A short-haired woman in a red coverall came over

to me. "Greetings! Welcome, honored guest! Where came you from?"

"Uh—" I pointed behind me down the corridor.

"Where belong you?" she asked. "Who your sponsor is?"

"Uh. . . ." How was I going to find Mark when I could hardly understand the language? Her words were English, but they didn't make sense!

"Come," she ordered, turning away from me.

The training kicked in. Without thinking, I followed her.

We headed along another narrow corridor choked with plants. This one was twisty, skinnier in places and wider in others. It seemed more like a cave than a building.

Then we came to a wall of windows. Outside, bright sunlight shone on a tropical view—palm trees, big tree ferns, all kinds of other weird-looking plants.

The woman went to a rack by the wall and pulled out two strange umbrellas. She handed one to me and opened the other.

Panels of dark see-through blue-gray plastic opened out in a circle on the end of the stick.

I opened mine, though I didn't know why. It wasn't raining outside.

"What's this for?" I asked.

"You know not UV protection?" She seemed surprised. "Always this put between you and the sun! Always, always! The UV, it your skin eats and your genes hurts!"

She pushed open one of the glass panels and we stepped out into even hotter, wetter air. It smelled like mushrooms and weeds.

People strolled by on white concrete walkways. Some rode bikes or giant scooters. Everyone carried umbrellas over their heads. And they were all amazingly tall. Every single one of them, women as well as men, could have played pro basketball.

They all wore colored coveralls, though some had patterns and stripes instead of just solid colors. How could they stand to wear long sleeves in this heat?

I gazed around. The buildings I could see through the haze were all made of the same slick blue stuff as the club building at home. Nothing looked familiar!

"Where *are* we?" I finally asked.

"Shadyside," the woman replied calmly.

Shadyside? "No way!" I protested. "Shadyside doesn't look anything like this!"

"Maybe not in your time," the woman said.

My time?

"Wh-what do you mean?" I stammered.

"Now is five hundred years later," the woman told me. "Know you not, child? Were not you told?

"This your future is!"

Chapter SEVENTEEN

The future!

"What?" I screamed.

Everybody in earshot clapped their hands over their ears.

I knew I wasn't home anymore. But *five hundred years in the future*? Five hundred years away from everything I knew?

How could it be?

"Five hundred years? What are you talking about?" I yelled.

That glass tube was a time machine?

"Quiet," the woman said when I paused for breath.

It worked again! I tried as hard as I could.

But I couldn't get any words out.

"Come," she ordered, and led me out onto the walkways.

We walked about a block through the stifling heat. It was like a jungle, with the huge tropical plants everywhere.

Then we came to a round blue building covered with vines. We lowered our umbrellas and ducked inside. The woman took mine and placed it in a rack. The air was cooler in here. Whew!

I blinked. When my eyes adjusted, they widened in amazement.

We stood in a huge, cavelike room. In front of me was a lot of machinery. It resembled the wirework and lacy silver stuff in the clubhouse building. But instead of being on the walls, it was heaped in castles and mounds that stretched from one side of the room to the other. Computer monitors blinked and flickered everywhere.

Then I spotted something horrifying.

A face. Right in the middle of one of the metal mounds.

"Whoa!" I gasped.

There was a human being in all this machinery!

Only her face was bare. Machinery, wires, and shiny colored dots covered the rest of her. I didn't think she could move.

Her arms were wrapped with silver lace. Wires

led from the ends of her fingers to connect with nearby machines.

I stared at her hands. She wore spiky silver gloves.

I remembered the machine that had turned into a glove on my hand, back in the clubhouse. If more of those machines had caught me, would I have ended up like this woman?

I felt sick to my stomach.

"Greetings," uttered a metallic female voice.

I was staring right at the woman's face, and I never saw her lips move. The voice came from the ceiling.

"Greetings!" answered the woman who brought me. "An unattached child here is." She patted my head. "What her assignment is?"

"Please hand present," directed the computer.

The woman led me over to one of the glowing screens in the middle of the machinery and pressed my hand to it. Red light shone from it for a second.

"Curious," the computer voice droned. "This child unassigned is. We must it package until we determine its origin."

Package me? What did that mean?

Wrap me up in plastic, like meat at a market?

"No!" I screamed. "*NO WAY!*"

The woman who led me there clapped her hands over her ears and squeezed her eyes shut.

It was the only chance I'd get.

Grabbing an umbrella, I dashed outside into the jungle. I raced along the walkway. I had no idea where I was going—I was just going! People stared at me as I ran by.

I didn't know what else to do. So I screamed at them.

They clutched their heads and backed away.

They must be totally not used to people screaming.

That was good to know.

I didn't know how to get back to the first building where the time machine was. But I didn't know what else to do—so I kept running.

I passed more buildings overgrown with vines and flowers. They all looked the same. The white cement walkways all looked the same. Even the people, despite their different colored coveralls, looked the same. Tall and pale.

Finally, I slowed down. The heat was really getting to me.

I should be looking for Mark. I didn't know how to find him though. Who could I ask?

If only I could find a future kid to talk to. But all I saw were grown ups. Not a single kid in sight.

I noticed the grown ups were approaching me, now that I had stopped screaming.

Uh-oh. What if they commanded me to stay, or be quiet, or sit, or something?

The nearest man opened his mouth. I was sure a command would come out. So I screamed.

He clapped his hands over his ears and hurried away.

I screamed until the nearest people ran away. Then I made a dash toward a jungle-like park.

The paths narrowed. Mushrooms big enough to sit on sprouted in the thick shade of big-leafed bushes and trees. Trees with huge flashy red and purple flowers on them sprouted everywhere.

I slowed again. Maybe I could find a water fountain. My throat was dry from screaming.

Then I heard footsteps on the path behind me. I ducked between a couple of trees and waited, too tired to run.

A short blond guy appeared.

He wore a dark purple coverall and carried an umbrella.

I watched him come closer and closer before I finally figured out—

He was a kid.

A kid I knew.

Trevor Dean!

I couldn't believe it! Where did he get those future clothes? Why wasn't he wearing highwater jeans and a too-small T-shirt, the way he always did?

I stepped out from the trees. "Trevor! What are *you* doing here?"

"Looking for you," he replied.

"What? How did you get here? How did you—"

"Quiet," Trevor ordered.

Just like that, my voice stopped working.

Trevor used one of the brainwashing commands on me!

What was going on?

"Come," Trevor ordered, grabbing my hand.

Another command! From Trevor?

Oh, no.

Suddenly I got it.

Trevor was one of *them*.

Chapter EIGHTEEN

Trevor Dean, a fink from the future!

"Come," he ordered again.

I couldn't stop my feet from moving. But I felt my throat open. I had my voice again.

Maybe I could still fight back!

"Sit!" I ordered Trevor.

He didn't sit.

He just gazed at me with pity.

"Quiet," he commanded. Then he added, "Those commands don't really work on me, you know. I just pretended they did."

My throat felt as if it were full of glue. I glared helplessly at him. What was he going to do now, package me in shrink-wrap? Stick my arm into a bin full of machines and turn me into a half-computer person?

We came out of the park onto a wide walkway. Trevor hurried me to another round building. He seemed very nervous.

I followed him inside. No computer person in the middle of a metal web here. Just a round lobby with oval doors opening off in four different directions.

Trevor led me toward a blue door. He tapped and the door opened. He dragged me through and closed the door behind us.

Potted plants sat between pieces of weird furniture. Most of it was brightly colored plastic stretched over metal frames. I guess you could sit or lie down on it, and use some of the rest for table space. But it sure looked uncomfortable.

The walls had silver lace in them, but not a lot.

In the far corner stood a tall, clear tube just like the time machine that had brought me here.

Trevor tugged me over to it.

What was the big idea?

Was he going to send me home?

Package me?

Or something even worse?

I wanted to ask. But my voice still wasn't working.

"In," Trevor commanded.

He shoved me into the tube—and pressed a button.

Chapter NINETEEN

My heart pounded. I waited for the sparkles to shine all around and blind me. Any second now, I'd end up—who knew where?

But it didn't happen.

Nothing happened. I just stood there, terrified. Trevor stood there too. He seemed to be waiting for something.

A second later a rectangular lavender package slid out of a slot in the room's wall.

Trevor picked it up and shook it out. It was a coverall.

Trevor opened the door of my tube and beckoned to me. I stepped out, wondering what was going on.

He handed me the coverall. "Put this on, or everyone who sees you will report you," he said. He went to the wall and tapped on it. Part of it slid aside. "Change in here."

I stepped through, bewildered.

I guessed the room he shut me into was a bathroom, but nothing in it looked like anything in any bathroom I'd ever seen.

The clothes didn't work with buttons or zippers either. I finally figured out that if you tapped some dark spots on the shoulders, the coverall opened up.

I put it on, tapped the dark spots again, and the coverall closed up tight. It fit me exactly. And it felt cool, not hot.

I tapped on the wall until it opened and let me out.

By now my throat didn't feel closed up anymore. "What is going on?" I yelled at Trevor.

He winced. "Not so loud. Please!"

"You better start talking, then," I warned.

"Okay, okay."

First he went to another place in the wall and tapped some buttons on the silver lace. A second later a compartment opened. He took two tall, iced glasses out and handed one to me.

My throat was so dry, I would have drunk anything. All that heat. All that screaming. I sipped.

It tasted weird, kind of a mixture of melons, tomatoes, and carrot juice. "What *is* this?"

"Total nutrition," he answered.

"Thanks. I think." I didn't like it, but I was so thirsty I gulped it down. Then I glared at Trevor. "So who are you?"

He sighed and sat down on one of the pieces of furniture.

"I'm Trevor Dean," he told me. "But I live here."

"Here, five hundred years in the future?"

"Right."

I folded my arms. "So what's the big idea of going back to my time and brainwashing kids?"

"The science council figured out time travel four years ago," Trevor began. "The Council of Twelve thought maybe we could get kids from the past. To help us with our problem."

"What problem?" I demanded.

Trevor sighed again. "In many ways, we are very advanced. As our computers got more sophisticated, they also got smaller."

"So what? Our computers are getting smaller too."

"But we now grow much bigger, much faster. Our hands are too big to do the fine work necessary." Trevor spread his arms. "Look at me. I've already grown six inches since I got to the past."

I stared at Trevor. Whoa! Six inches in two months? No wonder his clothes always looked too small!

"But wait," I protested. "What does that have to do with kids from our time?"

"Our climate control computers are breaking down," Trevor told me. He bit his lip. "But the only people here who have hands small enough to repair the computers are little kids. They're too young to handle the work."

"What?" I was so mad I could feel my face heat up. "You stole kids from the past to work on your dumb computers?"

Trevor winced. "When you put it like that, it sounds horrible," he protested. "We'll treat them very well. They get to live with us and be part of our families."

"It's still horrible," I retorted. "And what about all that brainwashing? What was *that* about?"

"You people from the twentieth century are so noisy and rude, we don't know how to handle you. We're very polite here."

I stared. "You need *polite* kids?"

"They fit in much better," Trevor explained. "First we tried going back to Victorian times. Everyone was *very* polite back then. But they didn't know anything about computers. So we had to try again." He hunched his shoulders. "We needed only ten kids."

"But they were training *everybody* in our class."

"That's how they start. They try to get everyone to join the clubs. Anybody who breaks conditioning too easily is dropped from the list. Like you. We never would have picked you. You were obviously wrong for the job."

"How come every kid thought the clubs did something different anyway?" I demanded.

Trevor shrugged. "Brainwashing works better on people who are happy while it's being done. They tap into the part of your brain that is just about being happy. You think you're doing your favorite thing while they're teaching you to obey orders."

"That's awful!"

"I guess," Trevor mumbled. He looked kind of guilty.

"But what about me? I didn't even know I joined a club! But I got trained anyway!" I cried.

"Sometimes they train people just to get them out of the way," Trevor explained. "They don't want snoopy kids figuring out what's going on and telling someone."

"But—but—" I sputtered. "*But they took Mark!*"

Trevor shrugged. "I was kind of surprised when Mr. Hool picked him. I guess he wrote a good essay. Kids who show an understanding of the importance of good manners are usually very trainable."

I sat for a minute, trying to take it all in.

"So why were you there?" I asked at last.

"They sent me back to, well, uh, help them select the best kids. Because I'm still the right size."

"What?" I yelled. He flinched, but I didn't care.

"You *helped* them steal kids?"

Trevor Dean was even more of a fink than I thought!

Bad enough our teacher was an evil kid-stealing mastermind from the future. Now this kid I thought was my friend turned out to be a spy too!

"Teachers don't see the kids when they're alone with other kids," he explained. "I was supposed to find out which ones were *truly* polite and nice, and which ones were putting on an act."

"So you hung out with me and Mark?"

"I, well, I wasn't supposed to do that. I was supposed to check out as many kids as I could. But—" He stared at his hands.

"But what?" I prompted.

Trevor's cheeks turned pink. "But I liked you guys," he mumbled. "You always seemed to be having fun. I wanted to be friends with you."

"Some friend," I grumbled.

After a minute he shook his head. "Anyway. You're here now, and you can't go back."

"What do you mean, I can't go back?" I wailed.

"They've already gotten the kids they needed from your time. Now they're cleaning up after themselves, making everybody forget those kids ever existed. You can't go back now."

"Oh, yes, I can! I'm going to find Mark and take him home!"

Trevor shook his head again. "Listen. I have nice parents, and I'm fluent in 1990s-speak. Why don't I get you assigned to my family? It would be fun. You could be my sister."

"No!" I yelled. "You help me find Mark—and then you help us get home!"

Trevor shook his head.

"If you don't help me," I warned, "I'll hate you forever."

"Not after you've been trained some more."

I stared at Trevor, shocked.

They could train me how to *feel*?

I hated the future!

"Come on, Trevor," I begged. "Please. If you really are my friend—help me! You don't understand how horrible it is to have someone else controlling your mind. You can't do that to me and Mark."

Trevor stared at me for a moment.

Then he stood up and went to the wall. He tapped something, and a computer screen popped out.

I swallowed hard. Was he going to help me find Mark?

Or was he going to turn me in?

Chapter TWENTY

Trevor tapped on his computer. I perched tensely on one of the plastic chairs.

Any minute now, the guys in pink coveralls might show up and take me away to be shrink-wrapped.

But I had to trust Trevor. There was nobody else who could help me.

Minutes went by. No patrol guys tapped open the door.

Then Trevor turned to me. "Mark has been assigned to live with High Councilor Mooluck."

I let out my breath. So he *was* going to help!

"He must have written a *really* good essay," Trevor added. "Only the best kids get placed with councilors' families."

"Mark is a good writer. And he wanted to go to Neverland so much." I shook my head. "What's going to happen to him when they find out what he's really like?"

"Oh, come on. He's pretty quiet. And his manners aren't *that* bad," Trevor argued.

I gave him a look. "You haven't seen him eat much, have you? He chews with his mouth open, he talks while he's chewing, he eats with his fingers. . . ."

Trevor's eyes widened. "Uh-oh. They'll send him in for more intense conditioning," he murmured.

"What does *that* mean?"

"The more you get conditioned, the less you act like yourself," Trevor explained. "And the more you act exactly the way they want you to act."

"That's horrible!" I cried.

"Yeah," he agreed softly. "I guess it is."

I jumped to my feet. "We have to go rescue Mark *now*! If they hate his table manners, what are they going to do when he burps?"

Trevor looked thoughtful. "When he burps?"

"Mark has total burp control! He can burp the alphabet! He's the only kid who ever beat Benjy Harrison in a burp-off."

Trevor grinned. "Mark can burp at will?"

"Anytime he wants," I said. "Why?"

"I just got a great idea." His smile grew wider.

"The Net says Mark is on a picnic by Fear Lake with Councilor Mooluck and his wife. Let's get over there right now."

Now that I was dressed in future clothes and knew how to twirl my umbrella, none of the grown ups we passed noticed me.

Trevor taught me to say "Greetings!" whenever anybody said anything to us. This made us practically invisible. I was glad I didn't have to scream anymore.

Trevor pointed out Shadyside Middle School when we passed it. I never would have recognized it otherwise. Not a single red brick showed on its big, lumpy, flowery face.

One thing hadn't changed though. Even though all the plants looked different in this time, they started getting scrawny and spooky-looking the closer we got to Fear Lake.

We hardly found enough bushes to hide behind near the water.

"Nobody but ghosts would have a picnic near this lake in my time," I whispered to Trevor.

"Nobody really wants to go here now either," Trevor murmured. "High Councilor Mooluck hopes to get people to clean this place up, so he comes here to make news."

I peeked between wilted fern leaves and saw a

man, a woman, and Mark sitting on a silver blanket. Mark was wearing a babyblue coverall. A big picnic umbrella stuck up over the blanket.

The man held up a large, insulated bottle. He poured orange liquid into three cups. Mark, the woman, and the man drank from the cups.

"Mmmm," Mark murmured.

They all gazed at each other and smiled as though they had just eaten the best fire-roasted hot dogs on Earth.

I poked Trevor. "*That's* a picnic?"

"Ouch!" Trevor rubbed his arm where I poked him. "Total nutrition," he muttered. "We eat real food only for supper."

So nobody had seen Mark's table manners yet.

"What do we do now?" I asked Trevor.

"All we have to do is get Mark to burp."

"What?" I stared at him. Was he kidding?

Trevor nodded, grinning. "Burping breaks the conditioning!"

I remembered how they had carried Benjy Harrison out of the training room after he burped.

Oh, boy! Finally Mark's burp power would come in handy!

"Let's just walk right over there," Trevor suggested. "We'll figure something out."

We lifted our umbrellas and strolled to the picnic blanket.

"Greetings!" High Councilor Mooluck said.

"Greetings!" his wife echoed.

"Greetings!" Mark repeated.

He looked *way* out of it. His eyes met mine and then moved on. No sign that he recognized me.

I shivered. Creepy!

"Greetings!" Trevor responded. I chimed in a second later.

"What you this beautiful day do?" Trevor asked.

"Picnic!" the councilor replied as if it wasn't perfectly obvious. "Please us join!"

"Thank you." Trevor and I sat down next to Mark.

I leaned over and whispered "Start swallowing air" into Mark's ear. I said it very firmly. Like an order.

Mark never even glanced at me. His eyes were glazed over. His face stayed totally blank. But he gulped.

"Swallow more air," I whispered again.

Mark never looked at me, but I saw his throat work.

"What say you, daughter?" the woman asked me.

"I said . . . supersonic burp, Mark!" I yelled.

Mark stared blankly ahead. I twisted my hands together anxiously.

Would he do it?

And then—

UUUUUUUuuuuuuuuuUUUUrrrrrRRP!

Awesome! A totally cataclysmic super-burp. Mark's best ever!

In the next second something amazing happened.

The councilor and his wife keeled over.

They'd fainted dead away!

Chapter TWENTY-ONE

Mark blinked and glanced around. He looked as if he were just waking up.

"Mark!" I cried. I felt like hugging him. "You're back!"

"What happened?" Mark mumbled,

"Come on," Trevor urged. He looked pale and a little ill. But he climbed to his feet. "We have to get back to the central building before they dismantle the time machine in your time."

"Huh?" Mark mumbled. "What's going on? Where are we?"

"We can't explain now. Come!" I yelled.

Mark jumped obediently to his feet and followed Trevor and me over to some scooters. We climbed on and raced back into town.

As we rode, I thought about the other essay-contest winners.

Actually, Trevor and Mr. Hool *did* pick out the most polite kids in our class. Except for Mark.

Elaine Costello, Gloria Badham, and Ian McDowell all used to come over to my house for *Strange Cases*. The other six were so nice, I hardly ever talked to them.

So they were polite. That didn't mean they deserved to be abandoned in the future and brainwashed until they didn't know their own names!

"Trevor," I called as we coasted along a walkway. "Wait. We can't leave yet."

"What?" He looked panicky.

"We have to get the other kids back too."

"We don't have time for that! You don't understand. Right now they're cleaning up the last memories anybody has of those kids and the clubhouse in your time. Then they're going to grab the time capsule in your time and bring it here. Pretty soon there will be *no way to get back*!"

I shrugged. "Then we'd better work fast. Because I'm not leaving here without those other kids."

Trevor gulped and nodded. "Okay."

We stopped at Shadyside Middle School. It looked totally spooky and deserted. Maybe there wasn't any school in the future. Maybe it was all on-line or something.

Trevor led us into the front hall and tapped on a cobwebby wall. A monitor popped up with a weird flat pad below it.

Trevor tapped the pad. It gooshed like a water bed. Letters flickered across the screen, too fast for me to read.

"All right!" Trevor cheered suddenly. "They're right here. In this building! Having a training session."

"Huh?" Mark muttered. He still seemed pretty dazed.

"Reinforcing their conditioning," Trevor explained. "We got lucky. This way!"

The halls were lined with dead plants. Only half the light panels worked.

We turned down another hallway. I felt the music through my feet before I heard it.

Fear rushed through me.

The music made me obey, too.

I was in danger here. They could make me do anything.

Maybe we should just turn around and get out of here while we still could! *If* we still could. . . .

Don't think like that, I scolded myself.

But I sure wished Mark had taught me how to burp on command.

"Burp!" I ordered Mark, just in case.

"UUUuuuurrrrp!"

111

Man, was he good!

The doors up the hall were open. The music grew louder.

"Sit!" ordered the voice of the training lady.

Before I knew what was happening, I sat on the floor!

Mark was still standing. I guess his burping helped him resist. I stared helplessly at him and Trevor.

"Stand!" the training voice ordered.

Now was my chance! I stood up—and ran to the door.

"Scream! Burp! Follow me!" I shouted.

None of these were training words. But the kids were all in brainwash mode. Maybe they would obey anyway. I hoped!

The training lady opened her mouth to give another order.

I screamed as loud as I could. She clapped her hands to her ears and stumbled backward.

"Burp! Come!" Trevor yelled when I paused for breath.

The kids turned around like zombies and lurched toward us.

Come. Right! That was a training word.

"Stop!" the lady commanded.

Everyone froze. Including me.

"Come!" Trevor screeched. "Burp! Scream! Come!"

Elaine let out a blood-curdling shriek. Ian belched. Then he shook his head and blinked. "Wha—?" he murmured.

"Burp again!" I yelled.

The other kids started screaming and burping too. They all shambled toward us. The training lady cowered in a corner of the room, covering her head with her arms.

"Come!" Trevor cried, leading us down the hallway.

I fell in step behind the others.

"Burp! Burp! Burp!" I yelled.

Mark belched again and again, to show everybody how it was done. Most of the other kids burped too.

The more they burped, the more they woke up.

Gloria let out a huge belch. *"Brrrrraaaaaaauuuuup!"*

I wanted to cheer!

We raced outside without umbrellas and ran like maniacs after Trevor.

By the time we got to the building where the time machine was, we were all sweating and out of breath.

I stopped. Everyone crowded around me, babbling questions. "Where are we? What's going on?"

I waved my arms. "Listen! If anybody tries to talk to you, scream as loud as you can," I instructed the other kids. "I'll explain everything later. Now let's go!"

We poured into the building. We smashed between polite adults, screaming whenever they tried to command us.

At last we made it to the time machine room.

Trevor popped down a computer monitor in the wall. He hit some keys. "The time module is still working," he said tensely. "But hurry!"

We shoved the other kids into the glass tube in pairs. Trevor worked the button. Finally Mark and I jumped in.

I paused, gazing at Trevor. He was a good friend after all.

It hit me that he was probably going to get in trouble for helping us.

"Do you want to come back with us?" I blurted out.

He shook his head. "Thanks. But I couldn't live in your time any more than you could live here," he answered.

I guess he had a point. But still, it felt weird to say good-bye to him forever.

"Thanks, Trevor. Thanks for everything," I told him.

"You're welcome. It was very interesting. And don't worry," he added. "I can handle things here. Ready?"

I nodded.

"Here goes." Trevor jabbed his thumb down on the green button on the control pad.

The air filled with sparkles. The floor hummed. My stomach dropped down to my shoes.

When the sparkles cleared, we were facing what looked like the same room. Except that it was full of the kids we saved from the future. And Trevor was gone.

Mark and I jumped out of the tube. The other kids surrounded us. "What happened?" Gloria demanded.

I opened my mouth to explain. But just then a long rumble shook the floor.

"I think we'd better get out of here," Mark warned. "This building is about to go."

The floor shook again.

"Run for it!" I yelled.

Chapter TWENTY-TWO

We tore through the ice-cube building. I pounded the front door and we all tumbled out onto Oak Street.

A second later the building folded up on itself and disappeared!

"Whoa!" I murmured.

It was the most amazing thing I ever saw.

Mark and I did our best to explain what happened to all the other kids. But I'm not sure how many of them really took it in. Most of them still seemed kind of dazed.

Probably just as well. It was a pretty wild story.

"I'm in big trouble," I told Mark as we walked home. "I just ran out of the house without saying anything. Right before dinner. I'm probably going to be grounded until I'm eighteen."

"What about me?" Mark demanded. "I'm supposed to be in Neverland with Mr. Hool. How am I going to explain *that* to my parents?"

I shook my head. "Good luck."

The yelling started as soon as I walked in the door.

"Valerie Martin, where on earth have you been?" my mom cried. "We've been going out of our minds with worry!"

"We've had the police out looking for you!" Dad exclaimed.

"I want an explanation. And it had better be good," Mom added grimly.

I opened my mouth. Then I shut it again.

What could I possibly tell them?

"Sorry," I mumbled. "It won't happen again."

"Is that it?" Dad demanded. "Is that all you have to say?"

I shrugged and flopped down on the couch. I felt exhausted all of a sudden.

"This is not acceptable behavior, Valerie," Mom said. "We're going to have to punish you."

I nodded. I figured that.

"No more *Strange Cases* for the next month," Mom said.

No more *Strange Cases*?

I couldn't help it. I started to laugh.

I didn't care if I ever watched *Strange Cases* again.

Life was so much stranger!

Turn the page to sneak a peek
at what's coming up next!
Escape of the He-Beast

ESCAPE OF THE HE-BEAST

Coming in June 1998

KABOOM!

Flames shot out from the computer monitor.

I threw my hands up to shield my face. A flying sliver of glass slashed across my knuckles. "Yeow!" I yelped.

Then the noise died down. After a second I cautiously lowered my hands.

My screen was shattered. Bitter-smelling black smoke billowed into the room.

The door to my room flew open. Mom and Dad raced in.

"What in the world—?" Dad gasped as he caught sight of my computer. He dashed out. A second later he returned with the fire extinguisher from the hallway. He began to spray my monitor.

Mom grabbed me by the shoulders. "Jamie, are you all right?" she demanded.

I coughed as a wisp of smoke drifted past my face. "I—I'm fine, I think," I managed to answer.

Dad put the fire extinguisher down. By now my monitor was nothing but a mass of white foam. Globs of it dripped down onto the processor.

"What happened?" he asked me.

I held out my hands. "I don't know."

"Well, what were you doing?"

"Nothing. I just turned on the computer and put a

disk in the drive," I explained. "Then my screen suddenly went nuts, and the whole computer started shaking. And then—kaboom."

It was the truth. Not the whole truth, maybe. I didn't mention that the disk I put into the drive was stolen from some weird kind of computer that I'd never seen before.

"Do you think it was some kind of virus?" I suggested.

Dad's eyebrows drew together. "I've never seen a virus that could make a monitor explode," he muttered. "But you never know with some of these hackers. They can do incredible things."

"Was it one of your comic book disks?" Mom asked. Her lips tightened. "Because I told you, no reading or drawing until *after* you finished your homework."

Uh-oh! I was about to get into even bigger trouble!

"No—it's just an old disk I had. I was going to save my book report on it," I lied quickly. "But maybe there was a bad file on it from before. Maybe it was something I downloaded from the Internet."

We carried my dead computer out to the garage. Then Dad set me up on his computer so I could write my book report.

It took me a long time. I'm a slow writer. I wish my teachers would let me draw my homework. It would be so much easier!

Besides, I had a hard time concentrating. I kept thinking about Refko's disk. And about my computer blowing up.

It was ten-thirty by the time I finally finished. I printed out my report, shut off the computer, and said good night to Mom and Dad. Then I trudged up to my room. I was beat!

I pushed open my bedroom door—and stopped short. My eyes widened in horror.

Between me and the window was a black shadow. A *moving* black shadow.

There was something in my room.

It was huge. Taller and broader than any normal human being.

A mane of bristling fur covered its head and neck.

It froze for a second when I opened the door.

Then it made a snarling noise and lunged forward.

It was coming after me!

About R.L. Stine

R.L. Stine is the best-selling author in America. He has written more than one hundred scary books for young people, all of them bestsellers.

His series include *Fear Street, Ghosts of Fear Street,* and the *Fear Street Sagas.*

Bob grew up in Columbus, Ohio. Today he lives in New York City with his wife, Janc, his son, Matt, and his dog, Nadine.

Don't Miss

R.L. Stine's
Ghosts of Fear Street #31

ESCAPE OF THE
HE-BEAST

He is Hecula the He-beast—the coolest monster in comic book history. And Jamie Kolker is his number-one fan. Jamie loves the He-beast's horns. His teeth. His claws. The way he hunts.

Then one day Jamie sneaks a peek at the computer program of the artist who draws Hecula. And somehow, he releases the comic book monster into the *real* world.

Suddenly Jamie isn't a fan anymore. He's monster chow.